Bus Stop Blues

4 Short Comedy Drama Sketches

2 Monologues

Melville Lovatt

TSL Drama

First published in Great Britain in 2020
By TSL Publications, Rickmansworth

Copyright © 2020 Melville Lovatt

ISBN / 978-1-913294-25-0

Cover courtesy of : https://pixabay.com/vectors/man-walking-confident-silhouette-2759950/ https://pixabay.com/vectors/silhouette-business-chair-woman-3264284/and Anne Samson

Contents

Monologues

Author's Note

The four short plays in *Bus Stop Blues* are independent of each other and can be presented separately or together in a complete programme of four.

An Update from Daphne

was first presented on
1 June 2019
as part of
The Harrow Writers Circle
70th Anniversary Evening
at
The Home Guard Club, Northwest London
with the following cast:

Daphne.........**Jenny Sutch**
Martin..........**Melville Lovatt**

Directed by Melville Lovatt

An Update from Daphne

A short play

Characters

DAPHNE - a woman in her forties
MARTIN - a man in his fifties

Running Time

5 minutes

Lights up.

A bus stop.

MARTIN *stands, waiting for a bus.*

He sighs, shakes his head.

DAPHNE *suddenly appears.*

DAPHNE: Has the H14 gone?

MARTIN: (*Looks up at her.*) Not yet.

DAPHNE: Good.

MARTIN: Should be here anytime. It's running late.

       Pause.

DAPHNE: (*Produces cigarettes.*) Do you mind if I smoke?

MARTIN: (*Surprised.*) No, we're in the open air …

DAPHNE: (*Offers cigarette.*) Do *you* smoke?

MARTIN: No. No thanks.

      Pause.

      (DAPHNE *decides against smoking, puts cigarettes away.*)

DAPHNE: (*Staring ahead.*) I've finally done it.

MARTIN: (*Looks up.*) Sorry?

DAPHNE: Just now. I've finally done it.

MARTIN: Done … done what?

DAPHNE: I *murdered* him.

MARTIN: (*Looks up.*) Sorry?

DAPHNE: Really *murdered* him.

MARTIN: Who?

DAPHNE: My husband.

MARTIN: You murdered him?

DAPHNE: Shut him up for good. Put an end to his boasting, once and for all.

(*Nods, pleased.*) Yes, I'm feeling quite pleased with myself.

Pause.

What a lovely evening. I love this time of year, don't you? When the leaves are beginning to turn?

Yes, the early Autumn's my favourite time of year. Those trees ... just *look* at them. *Beautiful!*

Yes, I've got an oak tree in my garden. I've just had it pruned. It's a joy to behold. Looks an absolute treat. Oh, the tree surgeon did a *wonderful* job.

He was dishy as well ... (*Quickly.*) but that's besides the point. (*Dreamily.*) Yes, I watched him in action from my bedroom window. So high up in the tree! On top of the world!

But when he came down, he was ever so cold. Poor thing. His hands were like two blocks of ice. But I soon warmed him up when I gave him his cocoa.

And we had a nice Swiss roly-poly as well.

Pause.

MARTIN: Getting back to your husband ...

DAPHNE: Our public servants are all really wonderful, don't you think?

Take our firemen, for example. Just think of what they do! They risk life and limb for us, putting out fires. I had a boyfriend who was a fireman, once. Looked a *picture* in his helmet. He never took it off ...

MARTIN: Getting back to your husband ...

DAPHNE: You're the first one I've told.

MARTIN: But why ... why tell *me?*

DAPHNE: You just happened to be here. I had to tell someone. Couldn't keep it to myself.

Pause.

(*Shrugs.*) So there we are.

Pause.

MARTIN: Let's just get this straight ...

DAPHNE: This bus is *very* late.

MARTIN: Just let's get this clear...

DAPHNE: Ah, here it comes, now. Oh no! An H12!

That's a fat lot of good! What's happened to the H14?

Pause.

MARTIN: Why did you do it, then?

DAPHNE: Sorry? Do what?

MARTIN: Murder your husband?

DAPHNE: Who said I did that?

MARTIN: Well, *you* did.

DAPHNE: (*Laughs.*) Just a figure of speech!

I murdered him at table tennis!

MARTIN: Oh ...

DAPHNE: He never thought I'd do it. He was always so smug every time he beat me.

(*Imitates her husband's north country voice.*)

'You've *no chance.* Give up. You'll never beat me. Why not give up now?'

So, unbeknown to him, I started taking lessons.

I practised and practised every afternoon.

Then, today the time came to take him on again.

Boy! What a picture! You should have seen his face!

He just couldn't believe it, how much I'd improved.

And not just my backhand. My forehand as well.

(*Mimes playing table tennis.*) Every time I used top-spin, I drove him right back. Had him running around like a blue arsed fly. Oh, pardon my expression.

I'm feeling so chuffed. From now on, this means I call all the shots. *I* decide when we do it. Not the other way around.

From now on we'll have *regular sex.*

Pause.

MARTIN: Regular sex?

DAPHNE: All part of the deal. We agreed, if I beat him, our sex life would change. And it *needed* to change, to put it mildly. He made endless excuses. Every single night.

(*Imitates husband's voice.*) 'I'm too tired. I've had a hard day at work. My back's playing up. Can we give it a miss? These new Statins are making my gums ache like mad and my foot's *really* sore. You know, I think I've got Gout.'

And so it went on. I was starved of affection. Our love life was going completely down the pan. Then I started getting headaches. *Terrible* headaches.

This *always* happens when I'm not getting -— (*Breaks off. Spots bus coming.*) Ah! Ah, here it comes now.

MARTIN: (*Glum.*) I need the H10.

DAPHNE: Poor you. Oh well, it should be along soon.

MARTIN: Look, *I* play table tennis. Do you fancy a game?

DAPHNE: (*Moves away to board bus.*) It's been very nice, chatting.

Cheerio!

Blackout.

Women in Trouble

was first presented in the
TSL Drama Showcase
at
North Harrow Community Library, Northwest London
on 26 October 2019
with the following cast:

Joyce...........**Barbara Towell**
Wendy.........**Gill Vidal**

Directed by Jennie Willett

Women in Trouble

A short play

Characters

JOYCE
WENDY
Both in their fifties

Running Time

5 minutes

Lights up.

A bus stop.

WENDY *and* JOYCE *stand, waiting for a bus.*

JOYCE: This bus service is going from bad to worse. I'll write a stinking letter of complaint. The pen is mightier than the sword, eh?

Tomorrow I'll write them a letter.

Pause.

WENDY: Oh, I didn't tell you …

JOYCE: Didn't tell me, what?

WENDY: Ken's not speaking to me. Not speaking at all. Now he's taken to sleeping in the other room. All because I mentioned the ceiling.

Pause.

JOYCE: The ceiling?

WENDY: Yeah.

JOYCE: What about it?

WENDY: Well …

JOYCE: *Which* ceiling?

WENDY: Our bedroom ceiling. I just … I just said it needed painting.

JOYCE: That's why he's not speaking? My God, what a delicate flower!

Pause.

He'll get over it. Can I make a suggestion?

It's only a ceiling when all's said and done. If he hates painting ceilings so much, then well ... get a decorator in to do it.

Pause.

WENDY: The thing is, there's a bit more to it than that ...

JOYCE: (*Emphatically.*) *Get a decorator in to paint the walls as well.* As it happens, I know someone very reasonable. Just give him a ring, and it's sorted.

Pause.

WENDY: Actually, Joyce, that wouldn't really sort it.

JOYCE: (*Emphatically.*) *A good decorator is worth his weight in gold.*

WENDY: The thing is, we were ...

JOYCE: What?

WENDY: (*Hushed, confidential.*) In the middle of something?

JOYCE: In the middle of something?

WENDY: If you know what I mean?

JOYCE: No, I don't.

WENDY: When I mentioned it? Mentioned the ceiling?

JOYCE: Where *is* this bloody bus?

Pause.

As it happens, Trevor's not speaking to *me.* Last night, he got a visit from the police. They didn't half give him a good telling off.

WENDY: What for?

JOYCE: Indecent exposure.

Pause.

WENDY: Indecent exposure?

JOYCE: He blames it all on me. You see, I'd only just cleaned the toilet with this special toilet cleaner which gets under the rim. So I stopped him using the toilet for a bit.

WENDY: Stopped him using the toilet?

JOYCE: Just for half an hour. But he couldn't wait, you see?

That's always been his trouble. He's never had *any* self control at all. So I made him go out to do it in the garden. I thought it was safe enough, there. But, *no.* What happens? He ends up getting reported.

WENDY: Who by?

JOYCE: Our next door neighbour.

WENDY: No!

JOYCE: Unbeknown to Trevor, she saw him in the garden from her bedroom window and reported him.

WENDY: Why?

JOYCE: She's *never* liked Trevor …

WENDY: How spiteful can you get?

JOYCE: I explained to the police about the toilet …

WENDY: They'd understand, surely?

JOYCE: Far from it. No. No, they just poo-pood it.

WENDY: (*Giggles.*) Poo-pood it?

JOYCE: So rude. 'We're not interested in silly excuses', they said. And then Trevor, silly sod, made things much worse. He got angry and started shouting at the police about what he'd *do* to our next door neighbour.

That was threatening behaviour, they said.

WENDY: Oh dear …

JOYCE: The thing was, he wouldn't … he *wouldn't* calm down. They had no choice, they said, but to take him away.

WENDY. (*Shocked.*) They took him away?!

JOYCE: Like a naughty little boy, he spent the night in a police cell.

Pause.

JOYCE: So, you see, you're not the only one in trouble. He's not a happy bunny at all.

(*Ponders, more to herself.*)

I'll probably decide to wear stockings and suspenders … That usually puts a smile back on his face …

(*Emphatically, faces* WENDY *again.*)

You see, *every* marriage has its ups and downs.

WENDY: My trouble is I'm not getting many … ups.

JOYCE: Just be thankful. Be thankful for what you've got. Your Ken runs a good business. He has strings to his bow.

WENDY: You make him sound like William Tell.

JOYCE: And your Ken's much better with people than my Trevor. Ken would never have ended up in a police cell.

WENDY: (*More to herself.*) I would never have sent him out into the garden …

JOYCE: Oh, I see. It's all *my* fault?

WENDY: All I'm saying is … well … with the benefit of hindsight …

JOYCE: Ah, *hindsight.* Yes! A wonderful word. Tell that to the marines.

WENDY: Look, don't get offended ---

JOYCE: So easy, isn't it? So easy to be wise after the event? For instance, if you hadn't mentioned the ceiling, Ken wouldn't be sleeping in the other room.

WENDY: Look, let's not fall out. At the end of the day, men are not worth falling out about. Right?

JOYCE: You can say that again.

Ah, here comes the bus. Here it is.

(*Shouts at the driver.*) Not before time!

They stand ready to board the bus.

Fade.

Going Out in Style

was first presented in the
TSL Drama Showcase
at
St John's Reformed Church, Northwood, Northwest London
on
9 February 2019
with the following cast:

TED...........**John Towell**
JASON.......**Graham Broderick**

Directed by Melville Lovatt

Going Out in Style

A short play

Characters

TED - a man in his fifties
JASON - a man in his twenties

Running Time

5 minutes

Lights up.

A bus stop.

TED *sits on a bench, sobbing, quietly.*

A small holdall bag lies by his feet. He wears an impressive designer label jacket. (Possibly leather?)

JASON *appears.*

JASON *stands a moment, unobserved by* TED.

After a while, the sobbing stops.

TED *wipes his eyes with handkerchief.*

Pause.

JASON: What's the matter, mate? You look a bit glum.

TED: (*Vaguely, looks at* JASON.) Have I met you before?

JASON: I don't think so. No.

TED: (*Suddenly stands.*) Then what's it to you if I look a bit glum?

I'm entitled to look as glum as I like!

In my position, *you'd* look glum too!

JASON: Steady on. Steady on. I only asked ---

TED: (*His face close to* JASON's.) I've decided to end it.

END IT! ALRIGHT?!

JASON: End what?

TED: MY LIFE! MY LIFE! MY LIFE!

JASON: Things can't be all that bad, can they? *No.*

TED: Well, son, they bloody well are!

TED *sits again.*

Silence.

JASON continues to stand.

They both stare ahead.

JASON: If you don't mind me asking ... *how* will you end it?

TED: Hanging.

JASON: Hanging?

TED: The rope's in this bag.

           I'm going to the woods to do it there.

           So ... so *don't* try and stop me.

JASON: No. No, I won't. If your mind's made up ... end of story.

           Pause.

TED: (*Exasperated.*) Where is it? This bus?

JASON: (*Looks at mobile.*) We've just missed one.

TED: Shit.

JASON: There'll be another one, soon.

           Pause.

           Actually, I think we *have* met before. You won't remember me, but I remember you. The jacket you're wearing, you bought it from my shop. Well, the shop I work in. Tk Maxx.

TED: (*Vaguely.*) Tk Maxx ...?

JASON: Watford branch. I work on the till. I remember the sale. About a month ago. Right? The sale was Gold Rated.

TED: What's that mean?

JASON: Well ... it was quite ... quite pricey? Reduced from five hundred?

A jacket like that's called a Gold Rated sale. I'm sure you remember buying it. Right? As it happens, I watched you. I could see you from my till.

(*Chuckles.*) Oh, You ponced around with it, something awful. You just couldn't make your mind up to buy it or not. Well, it *was* expensive. A limited edition from a top designer? Made in New York?

Well, you took the jacket off, put it back on the rail, (*Chuckles.*) then in less than five minutes, three guys tried it on as you stood back and watched. You should have seen your face! Yes, you thought you'd lost it. Lost it for good.

The third guy looked as if *he really would buy it.* Slung it over his arm, started walking towards my till. Then, against all odds, *he* changed his mind too!

Turned back and put it back on the rail. (*Smiles, shakes head.*) You were lucky to get that jacket, you know. Lots of guys tried it on. Have you worn it much?

TED: Twice.

JASON: You won't need it now, will you?

TED: How do you mean?

JASON: Well, you're going to the woods to hang yourself, right? There's nothing I can say to make you change your mind ...?

TED: Just sod off!

JASON: I can't. I'm waiting for this bus.

          (*Glances at mobile, groans.*) Oh no ...

TED: (*Looks at him.*) No, what?

JASON: They've cancelled it.

TED: What?

JASON: The bus. We're faced with a half hour wait.

TED: How come they cancelled it?

JASON: The driver's fallen ill.

TED: (*Groans, sits, head in hands.*) This is all I bloody well need.

   Pause.

JASON: (*Turns to* TED.) Look, about this jacket ... you're not going to need it.

TED: (*Adamant, stands.*) I'm hanging myself in this jacket today!

JASON: You've *finally* decided to go out in style?

TED: (*His face close to* JASON*'s.*) You trying to be funny?

JASON: I could make you an offer.

TED: What kind of offer?

JASON: A hundred quid. Cash.

TED: I paid nearly two!

JASON: But it's second hand now. It's been worn.

TED: Only twice.

JASON: Besides, you won't need it. Where *you're* going, you won't have any need for cash.

   So why not just donate it? Donate it to Oxfam? Alternatively, you could donate it to me.

TED: Why to you?

JASON: I'm ... homeless.

TED: Really? Tough shit.

JASON: Don't be heartless. If this is your last day on earth, you'll be doing some *good*. Think about it like that.

TED: Some good? Tell me why I should give it to you?

JASON: I'm your brother.

TED: My brother?

JASON: We're all … all brothers.

TED: How'd you make that out?

JASON: A brotherhood of man.

TED: Oh really?

JASON: Really.

TED: Then, how … how come …?

JASON: How come, what?

TED: Look, just … just go!

Pause.

JASON: In half an hour's time, it'll start getting dark. The drive to the woods takes three quarters of an hour … In practical terms, you might find you … (*Breaks off.*)

TED: What?

JASON: You might struggle to find a suitable tree.

By the time you get there, it'll … well … be pitch dark.

TED: (*Suddenly stands, decisively.*) One twenty, then.

JASON: What?

TED: The jacket's yours for one twenty.

JASON: A hundred's the best I can do.

TED: No, you're having a laugh.

JASON: A hundred quid. Cash.

(*Holds out cash to* TED.)

I can give you the money right now.

Pause.

(TED *quickly takes cash, stuffs it into jacket pocket.*)

JASON: The jacket?

(TED *unthinkingly hands over jacket with money still in pocket.*)

JASON: Thanks. You're still hanging yourself, then?

TED: Postponing it.

JASON: Ah.

TED: You're right. By the time I get there … too dark.

(*Starts to go off.*) I'm going for a pint in that pub over there.

JASON: You've forgotten something.

TED: (*Turns, faces* JASON.) What?

JASON: You've forgotten your rope. You can't hang yourself without that.

(TED *picks up his bag, goes off, right.*

JASON *swiftly slips on jacket, discovers money in pocket, gives himself the thumbs up, goes off briskly, left.*)

Blackout.

Bus Stop Blues

was first presented by
Player/Playwrights
at
The North London Tavern, Kilburn, London,
on
17 February 2020
with the following cast:

Doug.......**Philip Philmar**
Dave........**Clive Greenwood**

Bus Stop Blues

A short play

Characters

DOUG
DAVE
Both in their late forties

Running Time

10 minutes

Lights up.

Bus stop. Winter.

DOUG *and* DAVE, *shivering, waiting for bus.*

DAVE *looks at his watch, sighs.*

Pause.

DOUG: (*Looks at watch.*) The H14 should be along soon.

DAVE: We're better off waiting for the H12.

DOUG: But the H14 will take us halfway, and ---

DAVE: (*Impatient, quite sharp.*) Forget it. Wait for the 12.

           Pause.

DOUG: You alright?

DAVE: Sorry?

DOUG: You seem a bit …

DAVE: What?

DOUG: On edge.

DAVE: On edge?

DOUG: You seem a bit … stressed.

DAVE: I'm fine.

DOUG: How's Doreen?

DAVE: Doreen's fine, too.

DOUG: So everything's fine, then?

DAVE: Right.

           Pause.

Well, actually, Doreen's not really fine. The thing is, right now, she's going through the change.

DOUG: The change?

DAVE: Of life.

DOUG: Oh. Oh, I see.

DAVE: The thing is, with *most women,* it slows them down. Ninety-nine percent of women slow down. They just lose ... become less ... *they just slow down.*

Pause.

(*Glum.*) Doreen hasn't slowed down.

Pause.

The reverse has happened. She's gone sex mad. Wakes me up in the night. The middle of the night. I'm fast asleep, she starts scratching my back. Well, I mean ... it's no bloody joke. No. I told her. I need my eight hours sleep. I need my sleep like everyone else. I'm no spring chicken. I'm forty-eight. And it's not just nights. It's lunchtimes as well. Yesterday, it all just came to a head. I was out in the garden, digging all morning. Working my guts out. A boiling hot day. Sweat was pouring off me. I came in to rest. Dog tired, I was. In a state of collapse. I open the door and what do I find? She's waiting for me on the sofa. Yes! This was quarter to one! I was flabbergasted. I told her, I'm not a performing seal. I'm a human being. You know what she said? *Your trouble* is you're un-dersexed.

Pause.

DOUG: Perhaps we could swap.

DAVE: Swap?

DOUG: Swap wives.

DAVE: Swap wives?

DOUG: Why not? I mean, what can we lose?

        The thing is, I only get to do it at Christmas. Anne makes me wait for it, all the year round. With Anne, I promise you'll get *plenty* of sleep. And with Doreen, I might just be able to ...

DAVE: What?

DOUG: Slow her down.

DAVE: Slow her down?

        She'd slow *you* down. Can't believe what I'm hearing. You'd never stand the pace. You've a dodgy heart, Doug. You'd end up in a box. You're not serious, are you?

DOUG: Of course I'm not serious.

DAVE: Well, just for a minute ---

DOUG: (*Chuckles.*) You thought I was? (*Laughs.*) No!

        No, do me a favour. Can you see me with *Doreen?*

DAVE: I sure as hell can't see me with *Anne.*

DOUG: (*Suddenly offended.*) Oh, what's wrong with Anne, then?

DAVE: What's wrong with Doreen?

DOUG: (*Slowly, emphatically.*) *There is nothing wrong with Anne at all.*

DAVE: (*Shrugs, casually.*) No, she's just a bit frigid.

DOUG: Anne is *not* frigid.

DAVE: Once a year sex? Sounds frigid to me.

DOUG: Well, at least she's not a raving ... nymphomaniac.

DAVE: (*Angry.*) Now, *listen* ---

DOUG: Calm down. Let's not get excited. Love is horses for courses. *That's all it is.* Just horses for courses. As simple as that.

DAVE: You make it sound like the Cheltenham Gold Cup.

DOUG: Well, anyway, it's not worth us falling out, is it?

           (*Offers handshake.*) I hope we're still friends.

DAVE: (*Shakes hands.*) Of course. 'Course we are. Who needs women, anyway?

           (*Looks down the road.*) What's happened to this bus? Where *is* this sodding bus?

           Long Pause.

           Have you noticed something?

DOUG: Noticed what?

DAVE: This bus service. Lately, it's got a lot worse.

DOUG: Why is it, do you think?

DAVE: I know why it is.

DOUG: Oh, really?

DAVE: I *know* why it is.

           Pause.

DOUG: You gonna tell me, then?

DAVE: What?

DOUG: Why it's got a lot worse?

DAVE: It's happened since they switched to a *double decker bus* from a single decker. It's happened since then.

DOUG: (*Although clearly puzzled.*) Oh, *that's* it. Ah ... I see.

           Pause.

           Well, actually, *no.* I don't really see. The timetable's the same. There's nothing changed, there ... Double decker? Single decker? What difference would *that* make?

DAVE: Lots of difference.

DOUG: You've lost me.

DAVE: (*Emphatically, leaning close to* DOUG.) A double decker's more private.

DOUG: More private? More private for what?

DAVE: For the driver.

DOUG: The driver? You're talking in riddles. I don't really see how ---

DAVE: Okay. *Listen up.* The driver's last stop is not far down the road, but completely off the beaten track. Yes? It's the terminus, right? So when he gets there, there's never any passengers left on his bus.

(*Emphatically, leans close to* DOUG.) Except his girl-friend.

DOUG: His girlfriend?

DAVE: Right. She's waiting upstairs for him.

DOUG: No!

DAVE: Oh, *yes*. So he closes his doors for his twelve minute break, turns off his lights and joins her upstairs.

His twelve minute break becomes twenty-four min-utes. I've been told this on good authority ...

DOUG: (*Furious.*) So! Do you mean to tell me, whilst we're both standing here, freezing our socks off, waiting for his bus, he's having a bunk up on the top deck?

DAVE: You got it in one.

DOUG: Outrageous!

DAVE: Agreed.

DOUG: I'll have his head on a platter for this!

DAVE: Well, what you gonna do?

DOUG: Chief Executive.

DAVE: What?

DOUG: I'll write to the Chief Executive.

DAVE: Right …

DOUG: That's the only way to do it. Go straight to the top. I'll write a stinking letter.

Pause.

DAVE: (*After fiddling briefly with his mobile.*) Hello, we've got an update. A bus service update. They're saying the bus is running twenty minutes late due to engine failure.

DOUG: Engine failure? More to the point, his gear stick's got stuck.

DAVE: Oh come on, you're only jealous.

DOUG: Jealous of what?

DAVE: Him getting his oats and you not getting yours.

DOUG: But I *do* get my oats.

DAVE: Just at Christmas, you said.

DOUG: From now on, it'll be Easter as well …

Anne and me, we had a good man and wife chat. I told her how I felt in no uncertain terms. Once a year's not enough for *any* man, I said.

DAVE: Sometimes, with women, you've just got to be firm.

Pause.

Next week, Doreen's going to Cornwall for a week.

DOUG: To Cornwall?

DAVE:	On a spiritual retreat. *I'll* retreat whilst she's gone. Have a bloody good rest.
	(*Spots bus approaching.*) Ah! Here it comes, now.
DOUG:	At long last, eh?
DAVE:	*Will* you write to the Chief Executive?
DOUG:	Oh, yes.
DAVE:	Look, we don't want this driver losing his job …
DOUG:	Then he needs to pull his socks up.
DAVE:	And his pants.
DOUG:	Yes, well … don't worry. I *won't* mention that. I won't go into too much detail …
	Blackout.

Lights up.

Bus stop. Two weeks later.

DAVE *and* DOUG *waiting for bus.*

DAVE:	What do you reckon?
DOUG:	Reckon on what?
DAVE:	This bus service? I mean, it's *still* going down the pan. *Despite* your letter to the Chief Executive.
DOUG:	Well, you've got to give him time …
DAVE:	He hasn't even replied.
DOUG:	He will.
DAVE:	But when? It's been two weeks, now. I reckon you should have been much more precise.
DOUG:	How'd you mean?

DAVE: In your letter.

DOUG: Precise about what?

DAVE: About the driver.

DOUG: Look, we both agreed, we didn't want the driver losing his job.

DAVE: Even so, the Chief Executive must get lots of letters. Most of them boring. Commonplace complaints. But a letter implying one of his driver's is making the bus late, through having sex? *Well!* I mean, that's very different, if you see what I mean?

A letter like that would stand out from the crowd. It would grab his attention. Force him to act. A letter like that would make him prick up his ears.

DOUG: Look, things don't just change. Don't change over night. We have to be patient.

DAVE: Patient, eh?

DOUG: Look, if you're *so* unhappy, why don't *you* write?

DAVE: Alright, then. Alright. I *will.*

Blackout.

Lights up.

The following evening.

DOUG *and* DAVE *waiting for the bus.*

Pause.

DOUG: Did you write, then?

DAVE: What?

DOUG: To the Chief Executive? Last night, you said you were writing.

DAVE: Well …

DOUG: So I take it, you didn't?

DAVE: I'm writing tonight.

DOUG: (*Mutters to himself.*) I'll believe it when I see it.

DAVE: I *couldn't* write last night. The thing was, when I got home, Doreen was waiting for me. New nightie. Suspenders. The lot. I'm telling you, Doug, she's wearing me out. I can't wait for her to go on her spiritual retreat.

DOUG: I suppose the ideal is a happy medium …

DAVE: (*Reflects.*) A happy medium. Wonderful phrase …

DOUG: (*Sadly envious.*) *Some* men achieve it, a happy medium.

DAVE: No wonder I'm feeling tired all the time …

Pause.

Do you ever get the feeling everything's futile? That whatever you do is never enough?

DOUG: I'm so glad, Dave, that I met you tonight. I really did need a good cheering up.

(*Spots bus approaching.*) Ah, here he comes, now.

Our jolly bus driver. He's looking well. Lots of colour in his cheeks.

DAVE: I had an uncle who was a bus driver, once. My mum's twin brother. Uncle Eric. I remember, as a boy, when I got on his bus, he said, 'Look, you see all these people on my bus? Every single one of them bows down to me.'

I said, 'How do you mean? They bow down to *you?*'

He said, *'Watch.'*

Then he rammed the breaks on so hard …

DOUG: (*Laughs.*) He sounds like a right nutcase.

DAVE: King of the road. (*Chuckles.*) And they *really* bowed down. (*Recalls fondly.*) Yes, uncle Eric … Now he's driving his bus in the sky.

Fade.

First Love

Monologue

Character

VICTOR - a man in his early seventies

Running Time

5 minutes

Brief music. Eddie Cochrane's 'Three Steps To Heaven'.
Music fades.

Lights up.

VICTOR *stands, addresses audience.*

June 1960. I was twelve years old. Eddie Cochrane was number one in the charts. Every Friday night, my dad would give me threepence to buy a chocolate fudge bar from the Teddy Boy shop.

We lived in a long street of old terraced houses. This shop was on the corner of our street. It wasn't its real name, the Teddy Boy shop. But that's what we called it. We all called it that.

This was partly because it was run by a Ted, named Bob. He'd done time in Strangeways, Dad said. And the backroom had a big juke box in it with Teds and their girlfriends jiving away to Elvis, Gene Vincent, Little Richard, Jerry Lee Lewis with his Great Balls Of Fire.

'A week in the army! That'll sort 'em out!' Every so often, my dad would sound off. My mum was altogether more sympathetic: 'They're young, that's all. They need to let off steam.'

Well, nine times out of ten, I was in and out of the shop in less than thirty seconds flat. I'd pay Bob my threepence, walk out with my fudge bar.

Bob really was a man of few words. He would sometimes wink. I remember him winking. But I don't remember him saying much at all. Then I went there one Friday and Bob wasn't there. His daughter, Anne, sold me my fudge bar instead.

'Can you jive?' she asked, as I was turning to go. She was older than me. She was nearly fourteen.

I lied. 'Course I can. Of course I can jive.'

Well, the next thing I knew, we were in the back room, both jiving away with all the old Teds to 'Come On Everybody' and 'Summertime Blues'. I was hopeless, really. I'd never jived before, but Anne, as they say, took me under her wing. Taught me how to jive, proper. By the time she'd finished, all the Teds and their girlfriends started to applaud! They stood around us in a circle, clapping as we jived. I felt great! Really felt I was on top of the world!

But just as I was enjoying all this glory, who should appear in the doorway, but Dad. Face as red as a beetroot. Really angry. 'You have homework to do! Come on, get off home!'

The next thing I knew, I was being dragged out.

'Where've you been?' cried Mum. 'You've been gone for two hours!'

'I found him bloody dancing at the Teddy Boy shop! Well, I'll tell you this, sonny. You won't be going there again. There's some of those Teds have done time inside! Now get up to your room! Go on, now! Get up! Get up there and do your homework!'

For the next two weeks -— no more fudge bars for me. I was grounded. Doing maths homework in my room. It was summer. Quite hot. The window was open. Then one fine evening, a fudge bar flew in! Just sailed in through my window. Landed at my feet. I looked out, there was Anne, walking back up the street. I shouted out, 'Thanks!' But she didn't seem to hear. She just carried on walking back to the shop.

Well, from this point on, I couldn't stop thinking of her. I decided I just *had* to see her again, despite my dad saying, 'Stay away from that shop. If I catch you there again, you'll feel my belt.'

Thursday night, Mum and Dad went out to play Bingo. Or Housey Housey, as they called it back then. As soon as they'd gone, I climbed out my back window, leaving the window slightly ajar. The thing was, my parents wouldn't trust me with a key and I had to make sure I could climb back in.

This time around, I bought my own fudge bar. I remember Bob giving his famous wink. Then I peered through the back room and saw Anne jiving. Jiving away with a boy her own age. It was obvious she had eyes only for him. A Ted saw me, then yelled, 'Here, Anne! Here's your boyfriend! Your knight in shining armour has arrived!' And everyone laughed. Anne just carried on jiving. 'Come back for her when you've grown out of short pants! That was it. I went home feeling suicidal.

Well, no, maybe not, but I felt pretty low. When I got back, I found the house had been burgled. They'd got in through the window. My dad went berserk when he found out they'd nicked his record collection. When he'd finished, I couldn't sit down for a week.

Nothing happened for weeks after. Miserable, I was. Doing rotten homework. Night after night. Then, out of the blue, a second fudge bar flew in through the open window. A note attached to it, read:

Dear Victor,

Dad's selling the Teddy Boy shop. We're going to Australia to start a new life. Please remember me sometimes. I'm not all bad.

I promise I'll always remember you.

Anne.

Well, what can you say? I *have* remembered her. Often thought of her, down through the years. At twelve, I really thought she was the only girl for me. Even now, sometimes, I still do.

Fade.

The Dream
was winner of
The Harrow Writers Circle
Writing Competition 21 June 2018.

It was first presented in the
TSL Drama Showcase
at North Harrow Community Library
on 26 October 2019
with the following cast:

Raymond........**Melville Lovatt**

The Dream

Monologue

Character

RAYMOND - a man of sixty

Running Time

8 minutes

Lights up.
Silence.

Raymond stands, addresses audience.

She looked … very old. She stood by my feet. At first, she just stood … at the end of the bed. Her head … was turned. She was looking outside. I couldn't … couldn't see her face. No …

Then she turned. Turned towards me. Looked at me. Smiled. She moved towards me, slowly, smiling her smile. She was holding something. Something small. Something tiny. Glistened. Glistened in the dark. I couldn't see what it was.

She stood … quite still. Couldn't see her face, clearly. She had very long hair. Then she leaned … leaned over me. Over me … close. Her hand … holding something … moved … moved down … moved down … to my face … to my eye … my *eye* … A NEEDLE! SHE'S PUSHING IT … AAAAHH!

Fifty years ago today I was ten years old and had been having this same dream every night for three weeks. 'Just a dream. It'll go,' my parents said. But the dream didn't go. It kept coming back. And each time it came back, I saw a bit more.

Each time I saw a bit more of her face. 'Well, what shall we do?' I heard Mum say. They were downstairs, talking. The walls were wafer thin. 'Listen Norman, we can't carry on like this, can we? We need to get him some professional help.'

'How'd you mean?'

'A psychiatrist.'

'Do me a favour. Those people charge an arm and a leg! My wages won't stretch to that sort of thing. It's a *dream*, that's all. He'll get over it. Right?'

My dad had his own way of *making me get over it.* 'You're a bloody sissy. That's what you are. You're *supposed* to be a boy, not a girl. For God's sake, pull yourself together!'

Then, each night, before I went to sleep, he'd come in. Come in to my bedroom, sit by my bed and command me ... *command me* ... not to have the dream. *'You are never going to have this stupid dream again.'*

The thing was, Dad was a milkman, you see. I could understand him being upset. See, he had to get up at the crack of dawn. He really did need all the sleep he could get. And for one whole week, his tactics seemed to work. For a whole seven days, I didn't have the dream. Then one day, when I was walking to school, I *saw her. Actually saw her. Yes.* There were six old cottages next to the school. These cottages were in a terrible state. Due for demolition. Five were boarded up.

I just happened to glance over and there she was. She was sitting by the window of number six. I knew *then* ... I must have seen her in the window once before ... She was knitting ... knitting something ... using ... long needles ...

'I've seen her!' I told them. 'I've seen the old woman! Today I saw the old woman in the dream!'

'Well, that's good,' Mum said. 'And now that you've seen her, you will never have that horrid dream again.'

How wrong she was. The dream kept coming back. The same as before. Except every *other* night. Well, my mum and dad were never great readers. There were hardly any books in our house. Then, all of a sudden, we got a *new* book, *Confronting and overcoming your fear.* Now, Mum began reading this book all the time.

Dad said, 'You won't find any answers in *that.* If you want my opinion ---'

'I've *had* your opinion. You mocked him. Threatened him. Made him ten times worse!'

'Anybody would think this is all *my* fault. *I'm* the one suffering, make no mistake.'

'And I'm *not* suffering?'

'You don't have to go out four o'clock in the morning, delivering milk. In the freezing bloody cold, having had no sleep.'

'It might help if we meet her, like this book says ...'

'How'd you mean?'

'Might help him ... confront his fear ... It might help if we take him to meet this old woman. Once he's met her, he'll see there's nothing to fear. What is she after all? Just a harmless old woman.'

'I don't know ...'

'You don't know? Well, what do *you* suggest? It's affecting his school work and everything else.'

No one answered when Dad knocked on her door. We just stood there, quietly waiting for a while. Then Dad grew impatient. Started banging on her door. Just kept on banging the door with his fists.

'For God's sake, Norman. There's nobody in. We'll have to come back tomorrow. Let's go.'

Then just as we were going. Turning to go, we heard her voice. Her voice ... very faint. 'Go away. Go away and leave me alone.'

'Hello, we're sorry to disturb you,' said Dad.

'Go away.'

'Please open the door,' pleaded Mum.

'We don't mean you any harm. We just want a little chat. If you're busy tonight, we can call back again.'

'Go away and leave me alone.'

When we called back a second time, a few days later, after I'd had the dream yet again, her voice sounded even fainter. Dad lost his temper. Started shouting. But she still wouldn't open the door.

Over the years, I've sometimes wondered ... would it have happened if we *hadn't* called back? Was it *us* who pushed her over the edge? Would she *still* have done it? If we'd left her alone? They demolished the cottages very soon after, replacing them with an extension to the school. The property developer had been hounding her for years, to get her to leave. Or so the local paper said.

I wouldn't have done it, if I'd only known. Wouldn't have told Mum and Dad that I'd *seen* her. No. Still, what's done is done. It's all in the past. The past can't be changed. You're stuck with it. Right? All I know is I've never had the dream *since.* Since they found her ... the day after our visit.

Fade.

By Melville Lovatt

Full Length Plays

Small Mercies	Comedy-Drama	4M	2F
The Powers That Be	Thriller	3M	2F
Visiting Time	Family Drama	3M	2F
Desperate Measures	Dark Comedy	3M	1F

One Act Plays

Accommodation	Tragicomedy	4M	1F
The Lamp	Comedy-Drama	1M	1F
The Distressed Table	Comedy-Drama	1M	1F + Voiceover (F)
The Boomerang	Comedy-Drama	3M	1Boy + Voiceover (F)
Making Adjustments	Comedy-Drama	1M	2F
The Kiss	Thriller	2M	1F
The Weekend	Drama	2M	1F
The Grave	Drama	2M	

Bus Stop Blues

4 Short Comedy-Drama Sketches		1M 1F, 2F, 2M, 2M
2 Monologues	Comedy-Drama	1M, 1M

Duologue

Bedtime Story	Drama	1M	1F

Monologue Collections

Standing Alone (16 monologues)	Comedy-Drama	8M	8F

All enquiries to TSL Publications: www.tslbooks.uk

www.ingramcontent.com/pod-product-compliance
Lightning Source LLC
Chambersburg PA
CBHW070609180626
46817CB00005B/2061